The Girl with the Broken Wing

The
Girl
with the
Broken
Wing

Heather Dyer

illustrated by Peter Bailey

The Chicken House

SCHOLASTIC INC./NEW YORK

First published in the United Kingdom in 2005 by The Chicken House,
2 Palmer Street, Frome, Somerset BA11 1DS.
www.doublecluck.com

Library of Congress Cataloging-in-Publication Data available

ISBN 0-439-74827-5

10 9 8 7 6 5 4 3 2 1   05 06 07 08 09 10

Printed in the U.S.A.   37
First American edition, October 2005

The text type was set in 14-pt. Garamond.
The display type was set in Spumoni LP.
Book Design by Ian Butterworth and Leyah Jensen

Table of Contents

1
The Crash Landing

*Chimneys can be dangerous. Just imagine:
It's a dark night and you're flying low, barely
skimming the rooftops. The wind is gusting and
throwing you off course, and the rain is getting
in your eyes so you can hardly see where you're
going. And then, just as you're coming in to land,
there's a sudden gust of wind and — WHAM!*

The twins were in bed when it happened.
They heard a sound like a wet cabbage
hitting a wall, then a clattering on roof
tiles — then nothing but the wind wuthering
around the eaves once more.

"What was that?" whispered James.

Amanda, who slept behind a curtain on
the other side of the attic, switched on her
bedside light, and they lay very still, listening.

Rap rap! came a knock on the skylight.

"Who's there?" said James. He climbed out of bed and stood under the window, and there he saw a startled face framed by a tangle of windblown hair. "It's a girl!" he cried.

Together, the twins dragged the big red chair across from the corner, and James stood on it to reach the latch.

"Open up!" yelled the girl in a muffled voice.

James opened the window and a gust of rain blew into the room. "Thanks," gasped the girl, climbing in — and a moment later she was standing there before them, dripping on the carpet. To the twins' astonishment they saw that she was barefoot and wearing only a thin white cotton dress. But most astonishing of all, hanging from her shoulders and reaching nearly to her feet was a pair of long white wings.

"Ow!" moaned the girl, clutching her left shoulder. "I think I've broken my wing."

James and Amanda helped the girl with the broken wing to the sofa, where she sat down carefully. "I'll have to lie on my front," she said.

So Amanda brought a pillow and the girl lay down, with her long white wings folded neatly along her back. The tips of the wings lay on her calves, and the downy feathers at her shoulders were sticky with rain. Amanda reached out her hand and stroked one of the wings gently. It felt firm and springy, like stroking a swan.

"What's your name?" asked Amanda.

The girl with the broken wing yawned. "Hilary," she said.

"I'm Amanda," said Amanda politely. "And this is my brother, James."

"Nice to meet you," murmured Hilary, snuggling deeper into the pillow.

"Um — Hilary," said James, "what were you doing on our roof?"

Hilary mumbled something that neither of them could quite make out, then closed her eyes.

"Excuse me?" said James.

But there was no reply. Hilary's breathing had settled into the regular, easy rhythm of sleep.

"She's in shock," said Amanda. "We can ask her again in the morning."

Then, just as they were about to turn away, Hilary opened her eyes and spoke again — quite clearly this time.

"Good night!" she said.

2
The Angel Question

The first thing the twins remembered when the alarm went off was the girl with the broken wing — and there she was, still sleeping soundly on the sofa. They crept out of bed and stood looking down at her. She slept with one arm flopped over the side, and the wings on her back rose and fell gently with her breathing.

"Do you think she's an angel?" whispered Amanda.

James shook his head. "Angels don't snore," he said.

They watched her sleeping. Her elbow was skinned — probably from her crash landing the night before — and the soles of her feet were filthy.

"Perhaps we should wake her up," said Amanda.

James hesitated. Then he leaned down and said softly, *"Hilary!"* But Hilary slept on, undisturbed. James tried again, a little louder this time. *"Hilary!"*

Still nothing.

"HILARY!" he shouted.

Hilary's eyelids twitched but did not open.

"It's eight o'clock," said James, looking at his watch. "We've got to go."

"We can't just leave her."

The twins considered the situation. Amanda thought that they ought to tell their parents about Hilary, but James didn't think they should. "I don't think they believe in girls with broken wings," he said. "They might call the police or something."

This was true.

"Well, we can't throw her out," said Amanda. "Not with a broken wing. We'll have to hide her in our room and bring her food until she's well enough to fly again."

They looked at Hilary. She looked as though she could go on sleeping all day long.

"But what if she wakes up and goes downstairs?" James wondered. "Or what if Mom comes up and sees her?"

"We should leave a note for Hilary," said Amanda, and she ran to get her sketchbook and a green pencil, while James thought of what to say.

"Tell her we'll be back at four o'clock," said James.

There was a long pause while Amanda scribbled it down.

"And tell her not to go downstairs."

Amanda scribbled that down, too.

"And say that if she hears anyone coming up the stairs, she has to hide in the closet."

"OK," said Amanda. When she had finished writing, she folded the note and wrote HILARY on the front, with a smiley face. Then she put her sketchbook, some colored pencils, and a bag of chocolates next to the sofa, and balanced the note on top. Then they hurried down the stairs.

It's hard to believe that you've got a girl with a broken wing in your bedroom when you're bumping along in a school bus with people yelling all around you and throwing potato chips across the aisle. James and Amanda took a seat near the front of the bus to discuss her.

"Where do you think she came from?" asked James.

"Heaven," said Amanda simply. "That's where *all* the angels come from."

James grunted. "She doesn't look that much like an angel to me."

"How do you know? You've never seen one."

"I've read about them," said James. "They wear long robes and their heads are all lit up like lightbulbs."

"That's not their heads, that's their halos."

"And anyway," James continued, "angels don't really exist. If they did, you'd see them on the news."

James was a neat, logical person who parted his hair on the side and kept his things in boxes with lids. If there had ever been an angel in the news, he would know. Amanda, on the other hand, was the sort of girl who wore her long red hair in pigtails and sewed flower patches onto the back pockets of her jeans. Also, she read a lot of fiction, so she knew that *anything* was possible.

"And if she *was* an angel," said James, "what would she be doing on our roof?"

"Maybe she's a guardian angel," said Amanda. "They're the ones who get sent to Earth to help people."

James snorted.

"It's true!" said Amanda.

"OK, then," said James. "When we get home, we'll ask her point-blank and see what she says."

"We can't do that!" said Amanda indignantly. "Anyway — I *know* she's an angel. You're the one who isn't sure — *you* ask her."

"*I'm* not asking," said James. "Because I know she isn't. There's no such thing."

"There might be."

"There isn't. Ask anyone — ask a scientist!"

"All right," said Amanda. "We'll ask Mr. Lock at lunchtime. He'll know."

Mr. Lock was the teacher who knew the most about science. Whenever there was going to be something happening in the sky, like a comet or an eclipse, he always told his class so that they could go outside at night and look at it.

Mr. Lock spent his lunch hour in the back of his classroom, perched on a stool among heaps of broken Bunsen burners and empty brown jars. He quickly put away his sandwich when the twins came in.

"What can I do for you?" he asked.

"We were wondering about angels," said Amanda.

"Angels?" said Mr. Lock. "Is there a question about angels in the curriculum?"

"No," said James. "There isn't. We just wanted to know — could there be one?"

"A question?"

"No, an angel."

"Well now," said Mr. Lock, brushing crumbs off his white coat. "We'll need the blackboard for this one."

James and Amanda exchanged a weary look but followed Mr. Lock into the empty classroom.

$$x + y = z^2$$

12

"Are angels real . . . ?" said Mr. Lock, wiping off a lot of the calculations on the board. "Ah, yes . . . once upon a time that was the question *everyone* wanted the answer to, and a very smart man named Leonardo da Vinci looked into it. Observe . . ." He picked up a stub of chalk and began sketching.

"Da Vinci's theory was that in order to fly, an angel's wings had to be this big." Mr. Lock drew a man with enormous wings spread out behind him. "And to get liftoff, an angel's flight muscles would have had to have been supported by a breastbone *this* big." He drew an enormous sticking-out chest on the angel that looked like the one on a Thanksgiving turkey. "Of course, Da Vinci deduced that it would have been impossible," concluded Mr. Lock, turning to the twins. "An angel would have been way too heavy to fly."

"Oh," said Amanda, disappointed.

"What about a girl angel?" said James. "A small one?"

"Apparently," said Mr. Lock, erasing the angel with the turkey chest, "all angels are male."

So that solved it. Hilary couldn't be an angel after all — could she?

"Told you," said James to Amanda.

Amanda was not convinced, but she said nothing.

3
Hilary in Trouble

The afternoon dragged on. The twins couldn't help but wonder what Hilary was doing at home, and whether she would still be there when they got back. Neither of them could concentrate in their classes, and for the first time ever Amanda got in trouble for not paying attention. It seemed like forever before they found themselves back on the school bus and pulling into the stop at the end of their street.

"I hope she's all right," said Amanda as they stepped off the bus. "I hope she wasn't bored."

"Don't worry," said James. "As soon as we get in, we'll —" He stopped suddenly.

"Oh, *no!*" cried Amanda.

They could see Hilary from the bus stop. She was standing on the roof of their house in her thin white dress with her long white wings jutting out behind her — and she seemed to be throwing pointy white objects onto the lawn. Without a word, the twins rushed home and ran straight up the stairs — not even stopping to hang up their coats.

James jumped up on the red chair and put his head out through the skylight. "Hilary!" he hissed.

Startled, Hilary turned around. The front of her dress was smeared with chocolate, and there were paper airplanes littered all over the roof. *"Finally!"* she said. "Where have you *been*? I've been waiting all day for you two!"

"Get inside!" snapped James.

They waited while Hilary clambered back into their room, her arms full of paper planes. Then James let loose. "What do you think you're doing!" he cried. "Didn't you read the note?"

"What note?"

Amanda picked out one of the paper planes. It had green writing all over it. "*This* note," she said.

"I can't read writing," said Hilary, and she dumped the rest of the paper planes onto James's bed. "I can only read pictures."

"Only read *pictures*?" cried James.

"And music," said Hilary.

There was a shocked pause. "Well, reading isn't everything," said Amanda cheerfully. "I bet Hilary is far too busy to read — aren't you, Hilary?"

"Not really," said Hilary, and she flopped down on the sofa.

James and Amanda glanced at each other.

"So, um . . . what exactly *do* you do?" asked James.

Hilary retrieved a chocolate kiss that had slipped between the sofa cushions, and popped it into her mouth. "Not much," she said.

"But aren't you busy doing lots of — good deeds?" said Amanda hopefully.

"Good deeds?" asked Hilary.

"You know — helping people, that sort of thing."

"Oh, yes!" said Hilary, remembering. "Yes, I'm supposed to do *that*."

"I thought so," said Amanda, and she shot a triumphant look at James as if to say, *See? I told you she's an angel.*

James ignored it and turned to Hilary. "Exactly what sort of help," he said, "are you supposed to provide?"

Hilary promptly sat up straight, put her hand on her heart, and began to recite: "I promise," she said solemnly, "to love, honor, and obey, for richer or poorer, in sickness and in health, for as long as —"

"Isn't that what people say at weddings?" interrupted James.

"Oh! Yes," said Hilary. "It's not that one. It must be . . . I promise to think of others before myself and do a good turn every —"

"I know that one!" cried Amanda. "That's the Girl Scout code!"

There was a pause. Then Hilary sighed an exasperated sigh. "I don't *believe* it!" she said. "I've forgotten it *again*." And for a moment she looked so dismayed that Amanda felt quite sorry for her.

"If you could read," said Amanda helpfully, "you wouldn't have to remember it. You could just carry it around with you on a piece of paper."

"Mmm," said Hilary. "Maybe I'll learn to read when I go to school with you tomorrow."

"School?" said James.

"Yes," said Hilary.

James and Amanda looked at each other doubtfully.

"I'm sorry," said James eventually, "but you can't come to school with us."

"Why not?"

"Because you can't! You're not enrolled. You wouldn't like it, anyway."

"I would!"

"You wouldn't!"

"I would — I've *always* wanted to go to school," protested Hilary. "In fact, it's my most wanted thing in the *whole world.*"

"Well, I'm sorry," said James, "but there isn't any school tomorrow, anyway. It's the weekend. We're going to Beddgelert for a picnic."

"A picnic?" Hilary clapped her hands excitedly. "That's my *second* most wanted thing!"

4
The Wonderful Day

A s soon as the words popped out of his
mouth, James wished he'd never mentioned the picnic. But Hilary was persistent
and, like Amanda said, how could they deny
Hilary her second most wanted thing? She
would only be bored sitting at home, and surely
it couldn't do any harm if she came with them?

"But what about her wings?" said James.

"We'll disguise them," said Amanda. "No
one will know."

James was reluctant, but eventually he agreed to ask their parents if Hilary could come with them — provided her wings didn't show. At least then they would be able to keep an eye on her.

Of course, Mr. and Mrs. Mulroney were delighted to have the twins' new friend join them on the picnic. "The more, the merrier!" said Mr. Mulroney. "Have we met Hilary before?"

"No," said James. "She just moved here."

"Where from?"

"We don't know," admitted James.

Mr. Mulroney peered at his wife over his glasses. "Perhaps we should speak to Hilary's parents first," he said. "To make sure they don't mind."

"Oh, they won't mind!" said Amanda airily. "They'll never even know."

Mr. Mulroney stared at her. "What do you mean by that, Amanda?"

"Hilary's parents aren't here," James said quickly.

"Aren't here? Then where are they?"

"We don't know," said James. "We don't like to ask." This was true enough — and besides, as Amanda said later, Hilary was an angel, and angels don't have parents — do they?

"So if Hilary's parents aren't here," said Mr. Mulroney, "where is Hilary staying?"

"With friends," said James.

Mr. and Mrs. Mulroney exchanged a solemn look. It was their belief that families should stick together. They made a special effort to go on family outings and spend quality time together whenever they could — in fact, the Mulroneys spent so much quality time together that the twins sometimes felt it might be nice to have some quality time to themselves for a change.

"Well then," said Mr. Mulroney. "We'll speak to her friends instead."

This was clearly a difficulty, since Hilary's "friends" didn't have their own phone, but eventually it was decided to write them a note instead. James volunteered to deliver it. He was out and back again in a matter of minutes with the news that Hilary's friends had seen the note (he and Amanda had been there while their parents had written it, after all) and that it was all arranged — Hilary would come to the house first thing in the morning and join them on the picnic.

The twins got up especially early on the day of the picnic to disguise Hilary's wings. They found that when Hilary wore Amanda's old brown duffle coat, her wings were hardly noticeable. When the coat was all buttoned up, the wings were just a bump where her shoulder blades should have been, and when the hood was left down, it covered the bump quite well. The coat was a bit too big and the sleeves dangled over Hilary's hands, but the hem came right down to her ankles and concealed her wing tips perfectly.

"Hooray! Now shoes," said Amanda.

Hilary sat on the edge of Amanda's bed while they put a pair of heavy black lace-up shoes on her feet that James never wore. Hilary took a few faltering steps around the room, looking down at them.

"Walk properly," said James. "Or everyone will think there's something wrong with you."

"There *is* something wrong with me," said Hilary, offended. "I've got a broken wing."

James looked at her doubtfully but said nothing.

"And I don't like these shoes," said Hilary. "They're too heavy and they hurt my feet."

So they removed James's old black lace-ups, and Hilary sat on the edge of the bed while the twins went back and forth from the closet like salesclerks in a shoe store. They fitted Hilary with Wellingtons, then flip-flops, and then the strappy silver dress-up shoes that used to belong to Mrs. Mulroney. But nothing worked.

"These are all right," said Hilary, prancing around the room in the dress-up shoes.

But James said they weren't practical. "Don't we have anything else?" he asked.

Amanda rooted in the back of the closet once again until she found her old summer sandals, rather flattened.

"It's too cold for sandals," said James.

"Not if she wears socks."

So they buckled up the sandals over thick wool socks and told Hilary to take a few test steps.

"They fit!" she cried, and began skipping around the room in her duffle coat, singing, "I'm going on a picnic! I'm going on a picnic!"

James looked stern. "Hilary," he said. "You won't forget what we told you, will you?"

"About what?"

"About not drawing attention to yourself."

But Hilary was already standing on the red chair and opening the skylight — she was going to fly down (as well as she could

with a broken wing, she said) and ring the doorbell like an ordinary friend.

"Hilary?" said James. "Did you hear what I said?"

Hilary grinned. "It's going to be a *wonderful* day," she said. "I just *know* it."

James was not so sure.

The Mulroneys were going to have their picnic in Beddgelert, a little Welsh town that was famous for being the burial place of Prince Llewelyn's favorite hound, Gelert. It was a long way to Beddgelert and the winding roads made Amanda feel sick, but all the way there Hilary bounced up and down in the backseat and kept up a stream of questions. Mostly it was "Are we nearly there?" and the answer was always "Not yet."

But eventually they *were* there. It was a busy holiday weekend, and they found the little Welsh town teeming with tourists and day-trippers. The parking lot was nearly full.

"Here we are," said Mr. Mulroney, pulling into a space. "Beddgelert! That means 'Gelert's Grave' in Welsh, Hilary. Do you know the legend of Gelert? It's quite an interesting story. Gelert . . ." But Hilary had already jumped out and could be glimpsed running up and down excitedly between the parked cars.

James sighed. "I'll get her," he said.

They set off along the riverside. Mr. Mulroney stepped out in front with the picnic hamper, and Mrs. Mulroney brought up the rear in her hiking boots and floppy sun hat. She kept fanning herself with the map and saying, "What a scorcher!" But the warm day didn't seem to bother Hilary at all (despite her duffle coat), and she ran on ahead saying hello to everyone they met.

"Hilary seems to be enjoying herself," remarked Mrs. Mulroney.

"Hmm," said James uneasily.

At the very end of the path they came to

an oak tree with a group of people crowded around it.

"What are they looking at?" asked Hilary.

"Ah," said Mr. Mulroney mysteriously. "That would be Gelert's grave."

"Grave?" said Hilary, and she squeezed her way to the front of the group to peer at a slab of stone set into the grass. There was a lot of writing carved into the stone.

"What does it say?" asked Hilary.

"Well now," said Mr. Mulroney. "There lies a story."

"What story?"

The twins slumped; they had heard all their father's stories before. But Mr. Mulroney cleared his throat loudly and began.

"Many years ago," he said, and his voice rang out above the crowd, "Prince Llewelyn had a palace near here. Whenever he came to stay at the palace, he went hunting, and he always took with him his faithful hound, Gelert."

"Hound? What's a hound?" asked Hilary.

"A dog," said James.

"But on this day," said Mr. Mulroney, "Gelert wasn't with the hunting party."

"Why not?" asked Hilary.

"Prince Llewelyn had left Gelert behind to guard his baby son, who was sleeping in his crib."

"You mean — Gelert was the baby's *guardian?*" cried Hilary.

"Exactly," said Mr. Mulroney.

Hilary clapped her hands delightedly. By this time all the bystanders had fallen quiet and were following the story closely — and none more closely than Hilary.

"When Llewelyn returned from hunting," continued Mr. Mulroney, "Gelert ran down the palace steps to greet him — and to Llewelyn's horror he saw that the dog's jaws were *covered in blood.*"

Hilary gasped.

"Prince Llewelyn was very alarmed," said Mr. Mulroney. "He hurried —"

"Was Gelert bleeding?" interrupted Hilary.

"Shush," said someone in the crowd.

"Llewelyn hurried inside," repeated Mr. Mulroney, "to find his son. But the crib was empty, and —"

"Empty?" cried Hilary. "Where was the baby?"

"Shhhh!" said several people at once.

"The baby was gone," said Mr. Mulroney. "And the blankets and floor were covered in blood." Here he paused and glanced at Hilary, but Hilary was speechless. "Well," he continued, "Llewelyn put two and two together. He thought that Gelert must have killed his son, so he whipped out his jeweled dagger, raised it high above his head, and plunged it deep into Gelert's side."

"But —" Hilary objected.

"And then," Mr. Mulroney went on, "as Gelert gave his dying yelp, there came a child's cry. Llewelyn flung aside the blankets and found his son unharmed, and nearby was the bloody body of a mighty wolf that Gelert had slain."

There was a horrified silence.

Mr. Mulroney looked around at his audience. "Prince Llewelyn had made a terrible mistake. Gelert had not killed his son — he had killed the wolf to *save* his son." Mr. Mulroney shrugged. "They say Llewelyn never smiled again. And here is where he buried Gelert."

There was a stillness over the crowd; even the birds had stopped singing. A distant sheep bleated faintly . . . and then all of a sudden the silence was shattered by an anguished wail.

"Hilary!" said Mrs. Mulroney, shocked.

Everyone turned to look. Hilary's mouth was wide open and her face was red.

"There, there," said Mr. Mulroney. "It's only a story."

"It's not f-f-faaaaaair!" wailed Hilary.

The crowd began to murmur and disperse. Parents were taking their children by the hand and leading them away.

"How about some ice cream?" said Mrs. Mulroney brightly. But Hilary just shook her head in a silent wail, and a long dribble swung from the side of her mouth.

"Shut up!" hissed James, glancing around — but Hilary would not be comforted.

"I think we'd better go home," said Mr. Mulroney.

Hilary let herself be led away from Gelert's grave and back along the path. She sniffled miserably all the way to the car, causing everyone they passed to glance at her and shoot dark looks at Mr. and Mrs. Mulroney. "It's a *shame*," said one old lady.

James trailed behind them at a distance, with his hands in his pockets, hoping that no one would notice him.

All the way home, Hilary sat slumped in the backseat with her hood up; nothing they could say would cheer her up. She just kept sniffling to herself and muttering something about it "not being easy being a guardian."

It was a subdued group that arrived outside the Mulroneys' house.

"You go in and put the tea kettle on," Mr. Mulroney told his wife wearily. "I'll put the car in the garage."

But as they all got out, Hilary tipped back her hood and turned to Mr. Mulroney with a tearstained face. "Thanks, Mr. Mulroney," she said hoarsely. "I've had a *wonderful* day."

5
York Minster

"I *love* stories," said Hilary happily. Ever since the Wonderful Day, she had seemed content to sit on the sofa eating chocolates, wearing headphones, and listening to Mrs. Mulroney's audiobooks. She was so quiet that the twins kept forgetting she was there at all, and then were startled when she suddenly yelled out things like, "Don't do it, Mr. Elsewise!" or burst into gleeful laughter.

"Don't you have stories where you come from?" Amanda had asked.

"No," said Hilary. "We're not supposed to make things up."

No stories? The twins looked at Hilary inquisitively. "What's it like there?" asked James.

"Where?"

"Wherever it is you come from."

"Boring," said Hilary.

"But you must do *something*."

Hilary thought a while. "We sing," she said. "Hymns, mostly."

"Don't you do any dancing?" asked Amanda, who had just started taking ballet lessons.

"Sometimes," said Hilary. "As long as it's decorous."

"What's decorous?"

"Not moving your arms and legs too much."

James and Amanda glanced at each other. Poor Hilary! No wonder she was in no particular hurry to get back — it sounded even worse than school!

"What about sports?" asked James. "Don't you play soccer?"

"Oh, no! They're *far* too old for soccer."

"Too old? Aren't there any children there?"

Hilary shook her head. "Not as many as *here*," she said. And for a moment she looked almost sad.

Poor Hilary. Amanda supposed it was only to be expected that angels were mainly old people — but it couldn't be much fun for her, could it?

"Well, never mind," said Amanda eventually. "You can stay with us for as long as you like — can't she, James?"

But James just glanced at Amanda in annoyance and said nothing.

Then, one morning as the twins were getting ready for school, Hilary took off the headphones and said, "What are you doing?"

The twins looked at her.

"We're getting ready for school," said James. "What does it look like we're doing?"

"You don't normally take a water bottle," said Hilary, whose sharp eyes had missed nothing. "Or wear your weekend shoes."

"All right," admitted James. "We're not going to school. We're going on a field trip."

"You're going to a *field*?"

"It's not *in* a field," explained James. "We're going to York Minster, a cathedral. It's for our project and we're taking the train."

"Do they tell stories at York Minster?"

"No," said James. "They don't. And even if they did, you still can't come — not after last time."

"I won't ask questions," said Hilary. "They'll never know I'm there."

"They take a head count," said James.

"He's right," said Amanda. "They do."

Hilary begged and pleaded, but the twins remained firm, and by the time they left to catch the train, Hilary was sulking on the

40

sofa with her headphones on and wouldn't even say good-bye.

"I hope she'll be all right," said Amanda.

"She'll be fine," said James.

The train picked up speed, and the twins looked out on to the backs of unfamiliar houses; gardens growing right up to the railway line, ramshackle sheds, and overgrown banks of bindweed with its white trumpet flowers. Gradually the town thinned out and they were passing fields and telegraph poles. *Lickety-split, lickety-split* went the wheels on the train.

All of a sudden James grabbed Amanda's arm. "Ow!" said Amanda. "What?"

James pointed. High above the train and a little way behind, a dark speck was following. It was too big for a bird, too slow for a plane. It looked like a giant hawk, or one of those flying monkeys from *The Wizard of Oz*.

"It can't be," said Amanda.

But it was.

"She'll never keep up," said James. "It's miles to York."

They watched grimly, but Hilary seemed to be gaining on the train and dropping lower at the same time. Soon they could see her legs kicking like a person swimming the crawl, and her white dress billowing around her knees. She was carrying a bundle in her arms. "Your duffle coat," said James.

Fortunately no one else in the train seemed to have noticed her; they were too busy squabbling over their lunches. Hilary flew lower and lower until the twins lost sight of her behind the train.

"To the back," said Amanda.

They jumped up and ran shakily down the aisle, feeling like they were running the wrong way on a conveyor belt with the countryside flashing past in the opposite direction. In the very last car there was a window in the door. The tracks stretched behind them — empty. And so was the sky.

"Where did she go?" said Amanda.

In response there was a sudden *thunk* on the roof of the car, then the slap of sandaled feet running down the train.

"She's on the roof!" said James.

6
The Little Monk

When the train pulled in to York, Mrs. Stoke gathered everyone together on the platform. "Thirty-three," she said, counting heads. "Good. Follow me! Miss Evans will bring up the rear."

The twins looked around for Hilary, but she was nowhere to be seen. The roof of the train was clear, and they could see no brown duffle coat among the crowds.

"Have you two forgotten something?" asked Miss Evans.

"No," said James, and they hurried to catch up with the others.

There was a guide waiting to meet them outside the west door of the cathedral. "I'm Mr. Moffat," he said. He wore a brown suit and was bald on top with little white tufts of hair over his ears like a koala bear. "Keep together, everyone. And remember — sshh!" He pressed a finger to his lips.

It was dim and shady inside York Minster, like a great cave with slanted light coming in through high stained-glass windows. Mr. Moffat led the class through the nave, past rows of wooden pews, and waited while everyone gathered around.

"If you look to your left," said Mr. Moffat, "you will see the organ with its five thousand three hundred pipes."

Everyone looked left and saw the organ.

"And if you look to your right," he

continued, "you will see the crypt. Here lies the tomb of Saint Augustus, also known as the Little Monk due to his small stature. He was famous for his bell-ringing."

Everyone looked right and saw a room with low ceilings and pillars of stone where the bell-ringing monk rested. But Amanda was tugging at James's sleeve. "Look over there," she whispered.

James looked. Standing with a group of Japanese tourists admiring the angels in a stained-glass window, was a small, brown duffle-coated figure.

"Keep up, please," said Mr. Moffat.

The twins hurried to catch up with the rest of the class, and when they looked back again, Hilary was gone.

"Gather around, everyone," said Mr. Moffat. "Here we have the rose window. The rose window commemorates the —" He stopped suddenly. "Excuse me!" he said sharply. "You there!" And he pointed.

Everyone turned to look. Standing on

tiptoe at the back of the group was a girl in an oversized brown duffle coat.

"Are you with *us*?" asked Mr. Moffat.

Hilary looked around. "Who — me?"

"Yes, you! Where's your group?"

"She's not one of ours," said Mrs. Stoke.

"Shouldn't she be in school?" said Miss Evans.

Everyone stared at Hilary — everyone except James, who was pretending to be interested in something on the ceiling.

"Well, I'm sorry," said Mr. Moffat. "But you can't join *this* tour."

"I was only listening!"

"No listening allowed," said Mr. Moffat firmly. "Unless you're with the group."

"But —"

"I'm *waiting*," sang Mr. Moffat, ignoring the question.

There was a long silence, then reluctantly Hilary turned and shuffled off. Mr. Moffat waited until he thought she was out of earshot. "That's better," he said. "Now then —

over here we have the choir stalls. The acoustics were designed so that —"

"I can hear you!" came a thin cry.

The class looked around to see Hilary watching them from the other side of the cathedral.

"As I was saying," continued Mr. Moffat, "the acoustics —"

"I can still hear you!" This time Hilary was peeping out from behind a pillar, waving at them. The class giggled.

Mr. Moffat turned his back on her. "We'll do the ringing chamber and the bell tower," he said. He motioned for the class to gather around and waited until he was sure that Hilary had gone. Then he lowered his voice so that no one could overhear. "According to legend," he said, "the Little Monk used to ring the bells so beautifully that *angels* gathered on the roof to listen." Mr. Moffat paused dramatically and glanced upward, and the entire class glanced upward, too, as though they expected to see angels waiting for the bells to ring.

"Where's she gone?" James hissed to Amanda. Hilary had disappeared.

"This way," said Mr. Moffat. He started up a stone stairway, and the class followed behind him. Around and around they went, higher and higher. When they were about halfway up the tower, Mr. Moffat paused and cleared his throat. "In the ringing chamber, you will see the bell pulls hanging just as they did in fourteen —"

All of a sudden Mr. Moffat's voice was drowned out by a noise like a hundred pots and pans falling from a great height — and it was coming from the ringing chamber up ahead! Mr. Moffat gave an outraged yell and leaped on up the stairs.

Crowding into the chamber behind him, the class was confronted by a curious sight: A group of tourists were snapping pictures of what looked like a miniature monk swinging on the bell pulls.

"Check it out!" yelled a man in a safari suit. "It's a reenactment by the Little Monk!"

And there was Hilary wearing her duffle coat with the hood up. She was clinging to the bell ropes so, as the bells clanged, she sailed up into the belfry and then down again in front of the flashing cameras.

"Hell's bells!" yelled Mr. Moffat, rushing forward. "Stop that!" But Hilary had scuttled up one of the ropes like a monkey and set the bells a-jangling again.

Gradually the bells quieted and the ropes hung still.

"What goes up must come down," said Miss Evans, peering upward. Then all of a sudden something moved, and the crowd drew back as a dark shape came plummeting down toward them and fell to the floor at their feet — *thud!* Mrs. Stoke shrieked and Miss Evans covered her eyes and peeped through her fingers — but it was only Hilary's duffle coat!

So where was Hilary?

While everyone was staring at the coat,

51

there came a sudden down-rush of wind, and they all looked up just in time to see something swooping down toward them. Hilary flew straight over the balcony and into the cathedral, and then, like an angel in socks and sandals, she circled high above the astonished upturned faces. Once, twice around she went, then she dived straight downward with her white dress snapping and cracking around her calves. People below screamed and took cover between the pews, but Hilary shot straight out through the west door and disappeared.

There was a moment's silence, and then everyone began talking loudly. When no one was looking, Amanda picked up Hilary's duffle coat and stuffed it into her backpack.

Soon the police arrived. They said they suspected that the "Little Monk" stunt was some sort of student prank and everyone had to be questioned before they could leave. So the class missed the early train, and their dinner, and James never did get to draw the tomb of Saint Augustus for his class project — all because of Hilary. "What did she think she was *doing*?" he said. "I thought she had a broken wing?"

"She doesn't like being left behind," Amanda told him.

James just grunted. He didn't say another word all the way home.

It was eight o'clock by the time they got back, and they found Hilary sleeping soundly on the sofa as if she had never left it. "Wake up," said James, shaking her by the shoulder.

"Ow!" said Hilary. "Mind my wing." Then she turned over and fell asleep again.

" 'Ow,' nothing!" snapped James. "There's nothing wrong with that wing! Isn't it time you went home?"

7
The Angel Gabriel

"I don't think she's got a broken wing at all," said James the following morning while he and Amanda were brushing their teeth. "It's just an excuse."

"An excuse for what?"

"For not going home," said James. "She likes it here too much."

"Don't be silly," said Amanda.

"Well, it can't be much fun singing carols with a lot of old people, can it?"

"Hymns," corrected Amanda. "And she isn't here because she *likes* it. She's here to *help* someone."

"Help someone! What makes you think she's going to *help* anyone?"

Amanda sighed. "That's what angels *do*," she said. "Especially *guardian* angels — they help people."

James just spat into the sink and said, "There's no such thing as angels." And before Amanda could say anything else, he marched out of the bathroom.

But even James had to admit that Hilary had been on her best behavior lately. While the twins were at school she busied herself with drawing and jigsaw puzzles. She kept as quiet as a mouse so that Mr. and Mrs. Mulroney wouldn't suspect that she was there, and she was always so pleased to see the twins when they got home that it was hard to remain angry with her. Also, Christmas was coming, which always put James in a good mood. At school they were making paper snowflakes to decorate the classroom — and best of all they had started practicing for the Christmas play.

"I play a shepherd," James told Hilary proudly. "The one who speaks." He shook his script at Amanda. "Here — you be Gabriel."

Amanda took the script and found the place where the Angel Gabriel comes in. "DO NOT BE AFRAID," she read.

"Wait a minute," said James, who was putting his bathrobe on over his clothes. "You've got to fly in from the right and surprise us while we tend our flocks."

Amanda sighed, and went to conceal herself behind the curtain.

"BEHOLD," cried James, falling to his knees and raising his arms dramatically. "THE ANGEL GABRIEL!"

Amanda came running out from behind the curtain, flapping her arms. "DO NOT BE AFRAID!" she said. "I'M HERE TO —"

"Gabriel?" interrupted Hilary. "There's a part in your play for the *Angel* Gabriel? With *wings*?"

James sighed and let down his arms. "Percy's playing the angel," he said.

"Does Percy have wings?"

"His mom's making them," said Amanda. "Out of cardboard. She's sticking feathers on and —"

"Cardboard!" cried Hilary. "Cardboard's no good. Everyone will *know* they're not real."

"It's a play," said James wearily. "It doesn't *have* to be real."

"He'll never get off the ground!"

"He doesn't *have* to," cried James. "They lower him on a wire."

"A *wire?*" Hilary shook her head. "I don't think Gabriel would allow *that*," she said.

"It's all pretend," explained Amanda. "That's why it's called a play. You'll see."

But Hilary was not convinced. She went to sit on the sofa with her arms folded, and while the twins practiced James's lines she watched them thoughtfully.

By opening night, Hilary knew the script better than they did. She had been invited to accompany Mr. and Mrs. Mulroney to the school auditorium to watch the play, provided she behaved herself. "But remember to keep quiet," James told her, "and don't clap until the end."

"She's more excited than the twins," remarked Mrs. Mulroney. "And she's not even in it!"

Hilary just smiled and said nothing.

The play was sold out. The gymnasium had been filled with rows of chairs, the lights dimmed, and heavy red curtains drawn across the stage. While the orchestra tuned up at the front (Amanda was playing the violin, and she waved her bow at Mr. and Mrs. Mulroney), all the parents took their seats. Eventually the chatter and the rustling of programs subsided, and with a drumroll the curtains opened.

"It's a quiet night," came a voice from the wings. "Three shepherds tend their flocks."

The music teacher lifted his baton, and the orchestra started up like a rusty machine. Then onto the stage came three small shepherds, quite close together. All of them were wearing bathrobes and carrying walking sticks and had dish towels on their heads.

"Which one is James?" whispered Mr. Mulroney.

"The one with the poppies on his dish towel," replied Mrs. Mulroney.

The shepherds stopped in the middle of the stage and waited for their sheep (seven of the younger children), who came shuffling out after them on all fours with their woolly white tails and ears jiggling.

"Excuse me," whispered Hilary.

"Where are you going?" hissed Mr. Mulroney.

"It's my cue," said Hilary.

"What?"

". . . going to the loo," said Hilary. She edged past Mr. and Mrs. Mulroney and hurried out through a side door.

Now a yellow moon was rising on the back wall, and the light onstage was dimming. The shepherds put down their crooks and lay on the floor, and the sheep all huddled up together. The shepherd who was James yawned loudly and smacked his lips, and the audience chuckled. Then all of a sudden a very bright light shone down on the stage and the shepherds sat up, blinking and shading their eyes. "BEHOLD," cried the shepherd who was James, raising his arms dramatically. "THE ANGEL GABRIEL!"

James waited with his arms raised. Nothing happened.

"BEHOLD!" cried James again. "IT'S THE ANGEL GABRIEL!"

Still nothing happened. Then all of a sudden a mysterious winged figure wearing socks and sandals and a black mask launched herself onto the stage. She landed heavily and staggered a bit, but recovered and stood facing the astonished shepherds and their startled sheep.

"DO NOT BE AFRAID!" said Hilary, flinging open her arms.

There was a moment's hesitation, then, as one, the sheep clambered to their feet and ran shrieking off the stage. Two of the shepherds followed, letting their crooks clatter to the floor.

"DO NOT BE AFRAID!" said Hilary again. But it was too late — the sheep and shepherds had gone. Only James remained onstage. Hilary turned and beamed at him. "I AM THE ANGEL GABRIEL," she said.

The lone shepherd glared at the Angel Gabriel.

"I," said Hilary, a little more loudly this time, "AM THE ANGEL GABRIEL!"

"I HEARD YOU THE FIRST TIME!" yelled James.

The audience burst into laughter, and the shepherd who was James turned very red — but the Angel Gabriel wasn't fazed. She waited until the laughter had died down, then she turned to the glowering shepherd.

"I'M HERE TO TELL YOU," she said loudly, "THAT *A KING IS BORN TONIGHT!*"

The shepherd who was James scowled and said nothing.

"FOLLOW YONDER STAR," cried Hilary, and with one arm flung out toward the imaginary star, she sprinted across the stage, spread her wings, and leaped out over the audience. She circled the room once, twice, then disappeared into the lofty darkness of the gymnasium.

There was a moment's silence, then everyone began to talk at once.

"All done with mirrors, of course," said Mr. Mulroney.

Hilary returned to her seat after the intermission, a little flushed and out of breath.

"Where have you been?" asked Mrs. Mulroney. "You missed the best part!"

"That's OK," said Hilary, hiding a small smile. "You can tell me about it later," and she settled back contentedly to watch the second half.

But after the spectacular appearance of the Angel Gabriel, the play fell kind of flat. The orchestra seemed distracted, and whenever the shepherds came onstage, they brandished their crooks like weapons and kept glancing up at the ceiling. The sheep refused to appear at all.

Hilary enjoyed it though. "BEHOLD THE ANGEL GABRIEL!" she shouted in the car on the way home. "Mrs. Mulroney," she said, "tell us again about the Angel Gabriel. Was it the best part?"

Mrs. Mulroney admitted that the Angel Gabriel had been very good indeed. Everyone had loved it.

Everyone, that is, but James. He sat sulking in the back, his face turned toward the passing night.

"What's the matter, James?" asked his mother.

"Nothing," said James.

"Tell us again, Mr. Mulroney," persisted Hilary. "What did it look like when the Angel Gabriel came down and —"

"Shut up!" yelled James.

"James!" said Mr. Mulroney, shocked. "That's enough!" He turned to his wife. "I think," he said darkly, "we might have a *prima donna* in the backseat."

James scowled and slumped back into his corner, and all the way home nothing more was said.

No one could explain the angel. Everyone supposed that someone's relative had pulled the stunt — perhaps someone who worked in the film industry.

"I just feel sorry for Percy," said Amanda. "He still hasn't found his wings."

But James was furious. Hilary had ruined *everything*, he said, and he'd never forgive her. "There's nothing wrong with that wing," he grumbled. "When is she going home — that's what I want to know!"

8
Hilary's Treat

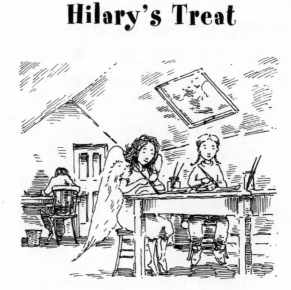

The following day it rained. Hilary and the twins were up in the attic, painting. That is, Hilary and Amanda were painting — James was sitting by himself at the corner table, coloring. He hadn't said a word to Hilary all morning and was stippling vigorously with the red pencil.

"I don't know why he's so upset," said Hilary. "It was much better with me in it. Much more *authentic*."

"He says you made him look stupid."

"He would have looked even stupider talking to someone on the end of a piece of string."

"Wire," corrected Amanda.

"OK, wire," said Hilary. She was thoughtful for a moment, then she leaned toward Amanda confidentially. "I know the *real* reason he's upset," she said.

James stopped dotting and looked up from his corner. "Why is that?"

"You're jealous," said Hilary.

"Jealous!" shouted James. "I'm not jealous! Why would I be jealous of *you*?"

Hilary smiled gently. "Because I can fly," she said. "And you can't."

James made an exasperated sound and started stippling again.

"But don't worry," continued Hilary. "I'm going to make it up to you."

James paused.

"Make it up to him?" said Amanda.

"Yes! I'm going to *treat* you — both of you."

"Treat us? How?"

Hilary smiled mysteriously. "I'll give you a clue," she said, and she put her arms out and started swooping around the room making a noise like an engine.

"What's that — a plane?" said James.

"No."

"Superman?"

"No."

"I give up," said James.

Hilary stopped swooping. "We're going *flying*, silly!"

There was a long, uncertain silence.

"What's the matter?" said Hilary. "Don't you want to?"

"Yes, but . . . how?"

"I'll carry you. We'll use a sheet," said Hilary. "It'll be just like when the stork delivers babies."

"You'd drop us," said James. "We'd be too heavy."

"I wouldn't drop you!" cried Hilary, offended. "I'm good at looking after people! Anyway, the difficult part is taking off. Once you're in the air, it's OK."

James considered the offer. "What about your broken wing?"

Hilary rolled her left shoulder experimentally. "It's much better now," she said.

James looked doubtful.

"Come on, James," coaxed Amanda. "Let's try it."

"Well . . ." James said. "All right then — as long as nobody sees us."

Amanda clapped her hands and jumped up and down. "When shall we do it?"

"Tonight," said Hilary. "After dark."

That night, when all the lights had been turned off downstairs and the rest of the house was quiet, they stripped the sheet from James's bed and spread it on the floor. Then the twins, all dressed and ready, stepped onto it and waited for instructions.

"OK," said Hilary, looking them up and down. "Now take off all your clothes."

"What?" cried the twins.

"Weight," explained Hilary. "We need to get your weight down."

"Well, I'm not going out with nothing on," said Amanda, stepping back onto the carpet.

"I'm sorry," said Hilary. "But I can't carry any extra baggage. Think how heavy jeans get when they're wet."

"They're not going to get wet!"

"They will if it rains. And look at your shoes — and those buttons. They all add up."

The twins thought about this.

"I'm keeping my shoes on," said James. "I don't care what you say."

"All right," said Hilary. "But you'll have to lose the rest."

There was an anxious silence. "I know!" said Amanda suddenly, and she went to rummage in her underwear drawer. She brought out something pink with yellow flowers on it and shook it at the others. "Swim-suits!"

Hilary took the garment in her hand and weighed it thoughtfully. "All right," she said.

"We'll freeze," protested James. But Hilary had made up her mind, so eventually James went behind the curtain to put on his swim trunks. He came back a moment later with his arms folded across his chest, looking very thin and very white, and wearing his good school lace-up shoes without any socks.

Hilary seemed satisfied. She even let them wear their woolly hats to keep warm. Then, as quietly as they could, they climbed out onto the roof and laid the sheet on the shingles. It was a cold, clear night, and the moon made everything look like a black-and-white photograph. The twins could see their breath in the air.

"Sit down in the middle," said Hilary.

The twins sat down side by side and waited, shivering with cold and excitement, while Hilary brought the corners of the sheet up around them and made a knot. "We'll never get off the ground," muttered James, his teeth chattering.

"Ready?" said Hilary.

"Ready," said the twins doubtfully, their woolly-hatted heads poking out at the top.

Hilary looped her arms under the knot and tested it. Then she spread her wings and with one strong wingbeat she was in the air above them; a second wingbeat and the twins felt the sheet straining — and on the third wingbeat they clutched each other and lifted off the roof.

"Help!" yelped James. (Later he told them he had just said "Well!" but it certainly sounded a lot like "Help!" at the time.)

"We're flying!" squealed Amanda.

The rooftops fell away below. From above, their house looked strange: the garden smaller, the garage at an unexpected angle. And as they climbed higher they

recognized other streets laid out below them, and the houses of neighbors, and the corner where the school bus stopped.

It was quiet up there except for the sound of Hilary's wings beating above them and the rush of wind past their ears.

"Are we heavy?" called James.

"No!" croaked Hilary. Her bare feet were kicking briskly, like a swimmer doing the crawl.

The ground was even farther away now, and the twins could see the lights of cars moving slowly along the roads. Hilary flew on.

"Where are we going?" called Amanda.

Hilary just grunted.

The twins could see that they were approaching the coast. The ocean glittered blackly in the distance, and they could see the lights of ships on the horizon.

"Look, it's Rhos-on-Sea," said James, pointing to the town just up ahead.

They seemed to be getting lower.

"Are we going down?" called Amanda.

"Umph!" said Hilary, kicking ever quicker.

They were definitely dropping. Now they could see individual houses and parked cars. Soon they could see into lit bedroom windows. Amanda saw a man closing the curtains.

"Are we going to land?" called James.

Now they were level with the streetlights; now with the upstairs bedrooms. Now they were flying down the middle of the road — and still they were dropping.

"I don't think we should land here," remarked James.

Hilary was still beating her wings and kicking valiantly.

"We might as well be walking!" cried James, for now they were barely skimming the surface of the road. A moment later, they touched down with a bump and found themselves sprawled on the road in their swimsuits.

"Ow!" said Amanda, nursing her knee.

James bundled up the sheet and glanced around angrily.

"Why did you put us down here?" he said. "Someone could see us!"

"C-couldn't help it," gasped Hilary. She was staggering around in the middle of the road, taking great rasping breaths and clutching her chest. "Too heavy. Must have been the shoes."

"I *knew* it," James said bitterly. "Now what do we do?"

"We're grounded," said Amanda.

And so they were. It was a cold night, and woolly hats aren't much help when you're wearing nothing but your swimsuit and school shoes. James wrapped the sheet around Amanda and himself and they stood there, teeth chattering, wondering what to do.

"I'll be all right in a minute," said Hilary. "I just need a high place to take off from."

"Great," said James sarcastically. "How about we knock on someone's door and say, 'Excuse me, can we just use your roof for a minute?'"

"If we could only find a tree . . ." said

Amanda. But it was one of those new housing developments where there are only small spiky bushes and flimsy saplings.

"We'll just have to turn around and walk back," said James. "Until we see something." And he and Amanda started walking, wrapped in the sheet. It felt like the time they went trick-or-treating for Halloween dressed up as a horse, only this time they were both the head.

"Wait for me!" cried Hilary.

So off they went — but none of them noticed the curtains twitching in the house across the road, or the lady with horn-rimmed glasses peering out after them with a telephone pressed against her ear.

9
Home Again, Hilary

"Which way now?" asked Amanda. They had walked what seemed like miles and seen nothing higher than a mailbox, and now they found themselves on a busy highway with cars whizzing past at lightning speed. As each car went by, the trio was illuminated in the headlights: the twins shrouded in James's grubby white sheet, and Hilary with her white dress and her long white wings.

"Let's keep walking," said Amanda. "Maybe

we'll pass one of those phones where you can call for help."

So on they went, picking their way along the shoulder of the road, with James muttering something like, "Great treat, Hilary. Thanks a lot."

It's only when you're walking along a highway that you realize how long it can be, and how boring. There were no landmarks up ahead to show them they were making any progress. It was like being in the desert. And deserts get cold at night, too.

"Let's run to keep warm," said James.

So the twins started jogging, with the sheet wrapped around them. They were just getting into the rhythm of it — left-right, left-right — when they heard the sudden swoosh of tires on gravel and turned around to see a car pulling off the road behind them. They stood blinking in the flashing blue lights as the door opened and the dark silhouette of a policeman got out.

"Hold it right there, kids," he said.

And, of course, they should have done just that. But when you're out in the middle of the night wearing only a sheet and your swimsuit and your parents think you're still tucked in bed, and when one of you has wings, you might be silly enough to do the first thing that comes to mind.

"Run!" said James.

So they did.

Officer Footit frowned and switched on his radio.

"569 to headquarters," he said.

"Go ahead, 569," came the crackling reply.

"I've found the kids," said Officer Footit. "They're heading down Route 55. I'm pursuing on foot."

He switched off the radio and started after them.

The twins stumbled along the shoulder of the road with Hilary right behind them, but they couldn't keep running forever. James was limping from a stone in his shoe, and Amanda was beginning to wheeze. Then, just as they thought they would have to stop and turn themselves in, Hilary cried out. "Look!" she said. "A bridge!" And with a sudden spurt of energy she sprinted down the road, spread her wings, and took off.

"Wait for us!" cried Amanda.

Not far behind them Officer Footit was fumbling for his radio. "569 approaching the bridge," he gasped, "in pursuit of . . . of —" Officer Footit stopped short and his mouth fell open. From where he stood he saw one of the small white figures lift clean off the ground, sail through the air, and alight on the top of the bridge.

"569?" came a far-off voice. "Do you copy? 569?"

But from Officer Footit's end there was just a static crackle in reply.

Hilary stood shivering on top of the bridge with her arms folded across her chest. "Hurry up!" she shouted to the twins. Then she noticed something strange — in the distance were the flashing blue lights of another police car. It was heading toward the bridge very slowly, and backed up behind it was a long line of traffic. That was odd. Then, turning around, Hilary saw a second police car approaching from the opposite direction — and it, too, had a line of traffic behind it. The cars came to a stop directly under the bridge, blocking both lanes, and four police officers jumped out of each police car.

"What's going on?" gasped the twins, joining Hilary at the bridge railing.

"I don't know," said Hilary.

"THIS IS OFFICER BAILEY," shouted one of the officers through a loudspeaker. "STAY RIGHT WHERE YOU ARE!"

"I think he means us," said Amanda.

Now people were getting out of their cars. They were slamming doors and coming down to the front to see what the delay was all about. Pretty soon there was quite a crowd of onlookers jostling for position at the front.

"Don't do it!" someone called.

"Do what?" said Hilary.

"Come on, Hilary. Let's go," said James. He and Amanda shrugged off the sheet, spread it out, and sat down in the middle. Hilary pulled up the corners and began to knot them.

Below, the officers were trying to get everyone back in their cars, but the crowd seemed reluctant to go, and there was a rising babble of protest. "YOU ON THE BRIDGE!" yelled Officer Bailey. "DON'T DO ANYTHING RASH!"

"Rash?" said Hilary. "What is he talking about?"

"Hilary!" shrieked Amanda. "Quick!"

Hilary looked around. Huffing and puffing and edging his way along the railing toward them was Officer Footit.

"Hurry!" cried James.

"Easy now," said Officer Footit.

Hilary tested the knot; then she looped her arms under it.

"Quick!" squealed Amanda.

Hilary spread her wings, and for one magical moment she looked from below like a marble angel, pale against the night sky. The onlookers gasped. Then with a single wingbeat she rose into the air, the sheet straining below her. With another wingbeat the heavy load was airborne. With one more beat of her wings she would have cleared the railing and lifted the twins up and out of reach — but she was too late. Officer Footit lunged forward and seized James by his dangling foot.

"Let go!" cried James.

Hilary grunted and flapped, but Officer

Footit held on bravely. Then, when it seemed that neither would give way and that James's foot was sure to come off, there was a sound like something coming unstuck, and Hilary sprang loose.

"We're free and clear!" she cried.

"No, we're not," wailed James. "I've *left my shoe behind*!"

And there on the bridge stood Officer Footit, gazing up at them with his mouth open, holding James's school shoe in one hand.

There was nothing Hilary could do but head for home. From the air they could see that they had already walked most of the way back and that the Mulroneys' house was only a couple of blocks away. Before long they had landed gently on their own rooftop and sneaked back in through the skylight.

"Well!" said Hilary, shaking the grit out of

James's sheet and putting it back on his bed. "All's well that ends well."

"It didn't end well!" cried James. "I lost my shoe! How am I going to explain that?"

"Tell your mother it fell off," said Hilary, "and you had to leave it behind."

James made an exasperated sound and climbed into bed.

"Or tell her that somebody took it," said Hilary.

James didn't answer but could be heard grunting and muttering, trying to get the rest of the grit out of his sheets.

"Good night, then," said Hilary.

"Good night," said Amanda.

"I'm sorry about the shoe, James." There was no answer, so Hilary tried again. "I didn't know you'd be so heavy," she said. "I thought . . . I thought . . ."

"You *didn't* think!" shouted James, throwing back the covers and sitting up. "That's why everything you do goes wrong!"

"But I only wanted to treat you to a ride."

"*Treat* us?" cried James. "I'll tell you what would treat us! If you went home again — now *that* would be a treat!"

10
Hilary Goes to School

There was a shocked silence. Then Hilary let out a sob and flung her face into the pillow.

"He didn't mean it," said Amanda.

"Yes, he did," said Hilary in a muffled voice.

"Tell her, James," pleaded Amanda. "Tell her you didn't mean it."

James sighed. "I didn't mean it," he said.

But Hilary didn't say another word all

night, and when the twins were ready to leave for school the following morning she was still lying on the sofa with her face pressed into the pillows.

"Come on, Hilary," said Amanda. "James doesn't *really* want you to go. Neither of us do." She shook Hilary's shoulder gently. "We've got to go to school now. Here — I'm leaving you my chocolates."

Hilary just mumbled something unintelligible and shrugged off Amanda's hand.

"Come *on*," said James. "We're going to miss the bus." So, reluctantly, Amanda left her chocolates on the arm of the sofa, and they headed down the stairs.

"Do you think she'll be OK?" asked Amanda.

"Of course she will," said James.

As soon as she heard the front door bang, Hilary sat up, put on her socks and sandals, and picked up her duffle coat. Then she dragged the big red chair across, opened the skylight, and climbed out. She stood on the roof for a minute or two and waited until the school bus had pulled away and was heading down the road. Then she folded her duffle coat over her arm, spread her wings, and took off after it.

There wasn't much traffic on the roads this early, and the school bus throttled loudly along, making lots of turns and stopping every now and then to let on more children. Hilary followed its meandering route and eventually, drifting up toward her on the breeze, came the clamor of the playground. Hilary's heart leaped. So *this* was where James and Amanda spent their day. It sounded as though they were all having an enormous party! Hilary frowned. Why should *she* have to stay at home alone while everyone else was down there having fun? It wasn't fair — she *never* got to have fun. Well, today Hilary would go to school like all the other children — and this time no one would stop her. With a flutter of excitement she circled the school once, twice, then started to descend.

Hilary touched down out of sight behind some garbage cans that smelled of potato peelings and old pears. She put on her duffle coat and smoothed her hair, then took a deep breath and stepped out from behind the garbage cans. At once she was confronted by a yard full of children all running around and yelling to one another.

"Hello!" said Hilary, waving shyly. "Yoo-hoo! May I . . ." But all of a sudden there was a deafening jangle and everyone started running for the doors.

"Hey!" yelled Hilary. "Wait!" But she was buffeted left and right as the kids surged past. "Where's everyone going?" she wailed. No one answered, and a moment later Hilary found herself alone in the playground as the last boy ran up the steps and in. The door banged behind him.

Hilary hesitated. She took one last glance

around the deserted playground and then she, too, hurried up the steps after the others.

Hilary found herself in a long empty corridor with doors down either side, and from behind the doors came the chatter of activity and the sound of chairs scraping back. The doors all had glass panels at the top, so Hilary went up to the first one, stood on tiptoe, and looked inside.

A woman with glasses on a gold chain was reading aloud. Hilary tried to hear what sort of story it was — but caught only words like "subtraction" and "division." Hilary had missed the beginning, anyway, and beginnings are always crucial to stories. Still — there were plenty more rooms to try.

In the next room Hilary could see children with their heads down, scribbling in their books. It didn't look very interesting, so Hilary moved on. She was just about to

peep through a third window when a door opened farther down the corridor and a lady came out.

"Hello," said the lady, looking at Hilary in surprise. "Why aren't you in class?"

"I'm choosing," Hilary told her.

"Choosing?" said the teacher, whose name was Mrs. Murray. "You can't *choose*. Who's your regular teacher?"

"I don't know," said Hilary. "It's my first day."

"First day! Hasn't anyone shown you where to go?"

"No."

"Dear me. What's your name?"

"Hilary."

"Hilary what?"

"Hilary nothing."

"Hilary Nothing," said Mrs. Murray slowly. "Hmm . . . It doesn't *sound* familiar. Never mind. Come with me."

She went to a nearby door, knocked twice, and entered.

Hilary found herself standing before a sea of curious faces, all turned toward her. There was a lady at the front with chopsticks in her hair.

"It's Hilary's first day," said Mrs. Murray. "Would you mind if I left her with you for a moment, Miss Lewis?"

"Not at all," said Miss Lewis, and she smiled at Hilary. "There's an empty seat over there. James will look after you. Won't you, James?"

Hilary looked around the room and to her surprise she saw James and Amanda staring at her from the back of the class. She waved cheerfully and made her way over.

"What are *you* doing here?" whispered Amanda.

"Going to school," said Hilary.

"You can't just '*go to school*,'" hissed James. "You're not even registered!"

"Quiet, please!" said Miss Lewis, glancing at James. "Today we are doing still-life drawings of fruit." With a flourish she unveiled a small table at the front of the class on which sat an orange, a plum, and a banana. "Paints or pastels, whichever you prefer. Hands up if you have any questions."

Everyone got up at once and started rummaging in the drawers and cupboards. Hilary looked around expectantly. "Isn't this exciting!" she exclaimed, and off she went to find some paints.

"She's gone too far this time," James said bitterly. "She's going to get us *all* in trouble."

"Just ignore her," said Amanda.

James scowled, but he got out his pencil and began sharpening it.

Soon Hilary returned with her supplies, and she sat down and started mixing colors and tinkling brushes loudly in her water jar. Then she stood back to look at the fruit and made some sort of measurement by squinting through her fingers.

James tried to ignore her. He shielded his paper with his arm and started drawing. He drew very carefully, with a lot of erasing when things went wrong. His picture was very small and very neat, and right in the middle of the paper.

Meanwhile, Hilary had started painting with big, sweeping strokes, getting as much paint as possible on her brush. Every now and then she would stand back to get a better look, then dab more color here and there.

"Very dramatic, Hilary," said Miss Lewis.

Hilary gave a blue grin. She had put the wrong end of the paintbrush in her mouth by mistake.

"And how are you doing, Amanda?" said Miss Lewis.

Amanda was shading carefully with yellow pastels. "Lovely! How about you, James?"

James, who'd been concealing his sketch in the crook of his arm, now had to show it. Hilary got up, too, and came to see. There was a pause.

"Very . . . tidy," said Miss Lewis.

"Aren't you going to color it in?" said Hilary.

"No," snapped James. "I'm not."

Miss Lewis moved on. Hilary went back to her painting, humming softly. James returned to his sketch. For a while, all was peaceful and the only sounds were of paintbrushes tinkling in water jars and pencils scratching gently. But before long, Hilary grew bored. "Finished!" she said, and she got up and started wandering between the desks, with her paintbrush in her hand.

"*Now* what is she doing?" muttered James.

Hilary was going around the classroom peering over people's shoulders and making comments about their work. "You've missed a spot," she said to Jeremy Short, taking her brush and dabbing at his picture.

"Hey!" said Jeremy.

James kept his head down and tried to

concentrate on his drawing. He was working on a very delicate part at the top of the orange — that little green star where it joins to the branch.

All of a sudden he felt Hilary looking over his shoulder.

"What's that?" she asked.

"What's what?" said James.

"That," said Hilary, pointing with her brush. And that's when it happened. A big blob of red paint chose that very moment to drop off the end of Hilary's paintbrush and land right in the middle of James's picture. It was such a big blob, and James's sketch was so small, that it nearly blotted out the whole thing.

For a moment neither James nor Hilary moved. Then all of a sudden James leaped to his feet and made a grab for Hilary's paint-brush. "Give me that!" he roared.

"James!" cried Miss Lewis, hurrying toward them.

There was a brief struggle. "Take it, then!" said Hilary, and she let go suddenly. But the moment she let go of the brush it flicked back toward James and red paint spattered all over his face. He let out a yell.

"James!" said Miss Lewis again. "Control yourself!"

"It's her!" cried James. "She does this all the time!"

"Does what all the time?"

But James couldn't answer. He was wiping his mouth with the back of his sleeve.

Miss Lewis sighed. "I'm disappointed in you, James," she said. "What sort of impression is Hilary going to get on her first day here?"

"I don't care," said James, defiantly. *She shouldn't be here at all!*"

There was a shocked pause.

"OK," said Miss Lewis. "That's enough. I want you to go to the principal's office right this minute, James, and tell him what you've done. Go on!"

Amanda could only watch in dismay as James threw down the brush and stalked out of the classroom, slamming the door behind him.

11
The Confession

James knocked softly on the principal's door.

"Come in," said Mr. Williams.

James had never been to the principal's office before. It was like a room in a house, with a big wooden desk and a sofa and a plant in one corner. Above the fireplace was a picture of a yacht.

Mr. Williams looked up. "James Mulroney,"

he said with some surprise. "What brings you here?"

"Miss Lewis sent me," James replied, looking at the floor.

"Did she, now? And why is that?"

James mumbled something.

"Excuse me?"

James mumbled something else.

"I see," said Mr. Williams. He pressed the tips of his fingers together and regarded James thoughtfully. "I think you'd better start from the beginning."

But before James could begin, Mr. Williams's phone rang. "Excuse me for a moment," said Mr. Williams.

James waited.

"Duffle coat?" said Mr. Williams. "Says her name is Nothing? No, she's not with me." He put down the phone and looked at James. "Wait here," he said, and he got up and went out, shutting the door behind him.

James looked around the room. He was just wondering whether it would be all right if he sat on the sofa when the door opened again and in came Hilary.

"All right," she said. "Where's the principal?"

"You can't come in here!" cried James.

"Don't worry," said Hilary. "I've come to confess. I'm going to tell him it was all my fault — even though it wasn't." She went and sat in Mr. Williams's chair with her sandals up on the edge of the desk and her hands behind her head. "I'll take *all* the blame," she said, sounding like one of the heroes from Mrs. Mulroney's audiobooks. "I'll be a martyr."

"A martyr?" cried James. "What are you talking about?"

Just then the door opened and in came Mr. Williams. "Hello," he said. "And who have we here?"

Hilary removed her sandals from the edge of the desk, stood up, and held out a hand. "How do you do?" she said. "I'm Hilary."

There was a pause. "Hilary?" said Mr.

Williams. He took her hand and shook it. "I've heard about you."

"Yes," said Hilary. "I'm here to confess. Please take a seat."

Mr. Williams sat down on the sofa and reached inside his jacket pocket. Then he hesitated. "Excuse me a moment, I need to make a phone call."

"Of course," said Hilary.

Mr. Williams took out his phone and dialed. "Yes," he said. "She's in my office. Right. Goodbye." And he put the phone away again.

"Sit down, James," said Hilary.

When they were both seated, Hilary sat back down in the principal's chair and folded her arms on the edge of the table. "There's been a misunderstanding," she said.

"There has?" said Mr. Williams.

"Yes. It was all my fault."

"What was?"

"Everything," said Hilary.

"I see," said Mr. Williams. "Perhaps you'd better start from the beginning."

But before Hilary could begin, the door flew open and in came Mrs. Murray, followed closely by Miss Lewis. "That's her!" said Mrs. Murray, pointing.

"She's not registered," said Miss Lewis breathlessly. "I've checked. And I've spoken to Saint Mary's and to Highbridge. They don't have a Nothing there, either."

Despite himself, James gave a snort of laughter.

"And what's the matter with you?" asked Mrs. Murray.

"Nothing!"

"All right, young lady, the game is up," said Mr. Williams sternly. "What's your real name?"

"Hilary!" said Hilary, bewildered.

"And what school do you go to?"

"I don't go to school!"

"Come, come," said Mr. Williams. "Everyone goes to school."

"I don't."

Mr. Williams frowned.

"Ask her where she lives!" demanded Mrs. Murray.

"Telephone her parents!" said Miss Lewis.

It was no use. Hilary could provide neither an address nor a telephone number, and when they asked her where she came from, she just pointed out the window and said, "From over there." Mr. Williams sighed and took out his phone again. "I'm afraid you leave me no option," he said. "If you won't tell the truth, I shall have to call the —"

"Wait!" said James, jumping to his feet. "It's true! She doesn't have a telephone. And she doesn't go to school, either."

The teachers exchanged disbelieving glances.

"And why," said Mr. Williams, "might that be?"

"Because . . ." said James. "Because . . ."

Everybody waited.

"Because she's . . . um . . ."

"Because *what*?" said Mrs. Murray.

James hesitated. "Because she's an *angel*," he said bravely.

For a moment everyone just stared at him. Then Mrs. Murray blinked. "I don't care *how* well behaved she is," she said. "She still has to go to school." She turned to Mr. Williams. "Let's look inside her coat," she said. "Maybe her real name is on the label."

"Good idea!" said Mr. Williams. And all three teachers began to advance.

"Run, Hilary!" shouted James.

Hilary saw an opening and made a dash for the door, but Mr. Williams was too quick. He grabbed her by the hood.

"Hold still," said Mrs. Murray, squeezing her fingers down the back of Hilary's collar. But this only made Hilary shriek and wriggle and shout that they were tickling her.

"Undo the toggles, Miss Lewis!" said Mr. Williams.

Hilary struggled, but she was no match

for the three of them. One by one her toggles came undone, and all of a sudden Mr. Williams found he was holding an empty duffle coat by the hood. And there was Hilary — standing before them in her long white dress with her long white wings standing out behind her. Her feathers were ruffled. All three teachers suddenly became very still, and their mouths fell open.

"I think you'd better go," said James to Hilary. And he went and opened the window for her.

"Thank you for having me," said Hilary. None of the teachers answered. Hilary stepped up on the principal's chair and climbed out through the window. She spread her wings and rose up into the sky, and before long she was just a small dark speck against the clouds — then gone completely.

A moment passed. Mrs. Murray sat down heavily in the principal's chair and asked for a glass of water. Miss Lewis rubbed her temples, and Mr. Williams realized he was still

holding Hilary's duffle coat at arm's length, as though it were something that had once been alive.

"I'll take that," said James politely, prying the coat from between the principal's fingers. Then he stepped outside and closed the door softly behind him.

When James had gone, there was an awkward silence. Finally Miss Lewis spoke. "Did anyone else see that?"

"See what?" said Mrs. Murray. "*I* didn't see anything. Did you, Mr. Williams?"

"Nothing at all," said Mr. Williams uncertainly.

The incident was never mentioned again. It was as though the teachers had all had a strange dream that they were too embarrassed to talk about. When Miss Lewis and Mrs. Murray had left the principal's office, Mr. Williams opened his bottom drawer, took a teaspoon of pink medicine, and then went back to work. Miss Lewis returned to class to find James working on a new drawing as if nothing had happened.

When the twins got home Hilary was waiting on the sofa, eating Amanda's chocolates. She jumped up and ran to James and threw her arms around him. "Thanks, James!" she cried.

James turned red and muttered something.

"Thanks for what?" Amanda said, surprised.

"Nothing!" said James.

"It wasn't nothing," Hilary said. "It was very brave."

"No, it wasn't."

"Yes, it was." Hilary turned to Amanda. "He told them I didn't have to go to school because I am an *angel*," she explained.

There was a short pause. Amanda looked at James, who was busy looking elsewhere. "Oh. Did he really?" she said slowly.

"And I didn't even get to confess," said Hilary ruefully. "Never mind. I'll make it up to him some other time."

James looked up, alarmed. "Oh, no!" he said. "You don't have to do that."

But Hilary just smiled. "Oh, yes, I do," she said.

12
Icky Vicky

"Vicky's coming tomorrow," said Amanda the following morning.

"Who's Vicky?" asked Hilary.

"She's our cousin," said James.

Vicky had been to stay with the twins before. She usually came with her parents, but this time Auntie Jean and Uncle Bob had won a vacation for two in Las Vegas, so Vicky was coming alone. And she wasn't happy about it. She said that there was nothing to do at the Mulroneys' house, which wasn't quite fair since the twins always *tried* to include her. But Vicky didn't like indoor games and she didn't like going outside, so it wasn't easy.

"Icky Vicky, we call her," said James unkindly. "Whenever she doesn't like something, she *says* she's allergic — but she isn't really. She says she's allergic to *everything*."

"Everything?"

"Not everything," said Amanda.

"Nearly everything," said James.

Hilary looked thoughtful. "She'll like *me*, though," she said. "Won't she?"

"Of course she will," said Amanda.

Vicky arrived the following day with two tight ponytails, one on either side of her head, and a little pink suitcase. "What's for dinner?" she demanded, putting down her suitcase and hanging up her coat.

"It's beans on toast," said Mrs. Mulroney. "You like baked beans, don't you, Vicky?"

Vicky made a face. "I'm allergic to beans," she said. "I only like the toast."

"I see," said Mrs. Mulroney, perplexed. "Well, go and say hello to the twins, and I'll call you when it's ready," and she returned to the kitchen to check on the cooking.

Vicky found the twins — and Hilary — doing a jigsaw puzzle on the floor of their room.

"Hello, Vicky!" said Amanda. "This is Hilary; she's a friend of ours."

"Hello," said Hilary.

"*Atchoo!*" said Vicky, and she went and sat on the sofa, drumming her heels against the baseboard. She didn't like new people.

"Do you want to do a jigsaw puzzle?" asked James.

"I don't like jigsaw puzzles," said Vicky.

She continued kicking her heels, and the others went back to what they had been doing. A little time went by and then Vicky pointed at Hilary and said, "Why is she wearing that ugly coat?"

The twins looked up.

"It's not an ugly coat!" said Amanda indignantly. (She had gone to school in that duffle coat for a whole year.)

Vicky did not reply. She got up off the sofa and went wandering around the room, picking things up and putting them down again. "What's this?" she said before long.

"It's a feather," replied Amanda. "It must be one of Hilary's."

"She *collects* them?"

"Sort of," said Amanda.

"Ugh," said Vicky, flicking it away. "I'm allergic to feathers. Get rid of them."

Hilary got to her feet. "Perhaps I should go," she said.

"No, you shouldn't," said James. "Sit down."

Vicky stamped her foot. "Get rid of them," she demanded. "*All* of them."

Hilary blanched. "I can't get rid of them *all*," she said.

"Then I will," said Vicky. "Where are they?"

"Here," said Hilary. And before the twins could stop her she got up, threw off her coat, and spread her wings. She flapped them a few times for good measure and sent a flurry of puzzle pieces across the carpet to settle at Vicky's feet.

"*Hilary!*" the twins cried together.

Vicky's eyes went very wide, and her face paled. Then she took a deep breath and opened her mouth to scream . . . but nothing but a high, hoarse whisper came out.

It took a while for the twins to calm Vicky down. Eventually they got her sitting on the sofa with a damp washcloth pressed against her forehead. Hilary put her coat

back on and was banished to the far side of the room, where she sat mulishly, watching the proceedings. "It's her own fault," said Hilary. "She asked me where my feathers were."

"Shut up, Hilary," said James.

Vicky eyed Hilary from under the wet cloth. "Do Auntie Jill and Uncle George know?" she asked.

"No!" said James. "And you mustn't tell them."

But Vicky was already struggling to get up.

"We mean it, Vicky," said James, pushing her back down. "You're not to tell *anyone* — all right?"

Vicky looked mutinous.

"Promise!"

Vicky pressed her lips together.

"Let her go," said Hilary from the corner of the room. "It doesn't matter who she tells. No one will believe her, anyway."

Vicky didn't tell — she just kept dropping hints. After dinner, when Mrs. Mulroney got up to clear the plates, Vicky followed her into the kitchen. "Auntie Jill," she said. "Why do you think Hilary wears that coat all the time?"

"I don't know, Vicky," said Mrs. Mulroney, scraping a plate. "Perhaps she likes it."

"But what do you think is underneath it, Auntie Jill?"

"I imagine Hilary is underneath it," said Mrs. Mulroney, laughing.

Vicky scowled. "I think she's *weird*," she said.

When the twins had gone back upstairs, Vicky tried Mr. Mulroney. "Look what I found, Uncle George," she said, twirling a long white feather.

"That's pretty," said Mr. Mulroney.

"Where do you think it's from?"

Mr. Mulroney lifted his glasses to take a

better look. "Could it be from a swan, do you think?"

"No," said Vicky. "It couldn't. It's not from a bird at all. And guess where I found it?"

"Where?"

"In the twins' bedroom!"

"Oh, well then," said Mr. Mulroney, replacing his glasses, "it's probably one of theirs. I would put it back where you found it." And he resumed reading his paper.

Vicky pressed her lips together angrily, and stalked back upstairs. Hilary was nowhere to be seen, but the twins were still doing their puzzle; it was a picture of lots of colored kites flying in the sky, and it was nearly finished. Vicky sat on the sofa and watched them for a moment.

"They'll find out sooner or later," she said.

"Find out what?" Amanda said.

"About the *wings*."

James sat back on his heels and looked at Vicky. "And how would that happen?"

Vicky shrugged. "One day," she said, "she'll *have* to take off her coat."

"Why?"

"Well — what if someone's hair caught fire," said Vicky, "and she had to smother the flames with her coat?"

"Don't be ridiculous," said Amanda.

"Or what if she had to catch a baby falling from a skyscraper?" Vicky went on. "She'd have to take it off then, wouldn't she?"

"What — like Superman?" said James. "There aren't any skyscrapers around here."

"All right, then — what if someone was being *blown away*," persisted Vicky, turning a piece of red kite over and over in her fingers. "Like if they were holding on to something *really big* that pulled them into the sky. It *could* happen," she went on, almost to herself. "If the person wasn't too heavy, and if his or her hand was tangled in the string . . . Hilary would have to take the coat off then, wouldn't she? To fly to the rescue?"

126

"What?" said James impatiently. "Yes, maybe . . . Look! There's one piece missing."

Vicky smiled to herself and pressed the last corner of the red kite into place.

13
The Enormous Kite

"**G**ood grief!" cried Mr. Mulroney. "What on Earth is that?"

"It's a kite," said Vicky.

"But it's enormous!"

"Yep," said Vicky. She had borrowed an old sheet and the poles from the Mulroneys' tent, and had spent all afternoon cutting and sewing. Now that the kite was spread out on the floor, it filled the whole room. There was a long tail of red ribbon, a ball of string to fly it with, and painted right across it was a great big grinning face.

"Can we go and fly it?" asked Vicky.

Mr. Mulroney looked doubtful.

"Pleeeease," said Vicky.

"Well, all right," said Mr. Mulroney. "If we can get it on top of the car."

"Good," said Vicky. "Can Hilary come, too?"

With help from the whole family, including Hilary, Mr. Mulroney managed to get the kite on the roof rack and lash it down with ropes. Then they all got into the car and off they went, with the enormous kite grinning garishly and all the neighbors staring after them.

"This is stupid," muttered James.

As they picked up speed the kite riffled loudly in the wind like the pages of a book, and by the time they got on the expressway it was so loud that they could barely hear themselves speak.

"DO YOU THINK IT'LL FLY?" shouted Vicky.

"DEFINITELY," yelled Hilary.

Vicky smiled and settled back into her seat.

When they got to the park, they stepped out of the car into bright sunshine and a gusty wind. Mr. and Mrs. Mulroney spread out the picnic blanket and sat down.

"Go and help Vicky fly her kite," said Mr. Mulroney. "She made it especially for today."

"If we have to," grumbled James.

Hilary and Amanda laid the kite on the grass. They had to kneel on it to keep it down, for it flapped and snapped in the breeze like a live thing. Then James and Vicky unraveled the string a good distance.

"What's taking them so long?" said Hilary. From where she and Amanda were kneeling it looked as if Vicky were teaching James to wind the string around his wrists . . .

"I don't know," said Amanda. "But I wish they'd hurry up."

"I'll go and help," said Hilary. She got up and started toward them — but the moment she stood up, the wind caught her side of the kite and lifted it.

"Wait!" cried Amanda, struggling to hold it down. But she was no match for the enormous kite. With a sudden gust it bucked her off and rose straight up into the sky, its painted face leering down in triumph. But that wasn't all. With a yell, James was yanked forward by his wrists. "Help!" he wailed, staggering after it. But the kite was gathering speed, and soon James's feet were barely touching the ground.

"Oh, dear," said Vicky, smirking.

"Quick!" yelled Amanda.

But before they could catch up with him, James was airborne. "After him!" cried Mr. Mulroney, pounding past, followed closely by Mrs. Mulroney and Amanda.

Only Vicky and Hilary stayed where they were. Vicky turned to Hilary. "Well," she said, "you should *help* him, shouldn't you?" She smiled unpleasantly.

Hilary did not reply. She waited until no one was looking, then she slipped off her duffle coat and slung it over one arm, spread her wings, and rose gracefully into the air.

The kite was now high above the park. The wind jigged it this way and that, and like a trapeze artist on the end of a rope, James swung from side to side. A faint wail drifted down.

The Mulroneys ran at top speed across the field, past the swings and the picnic area, and everywhere they went people stopped what they were doing and joined in the chase. Eventually there was a long line of people (and dogs, and a lady pushing a jog-gling baby in a carriage), all keen to see where the kite might land. And the whole time, the grinning kite drifted on above them, with James dangling beneath.

But now the kite was heading toward a cluster of tall elms. For an anxious moment James's foot snagged in the top of the tallest tree — but then the kite tugged him free

again and began sinking toward the boating pond on the other side.

"Quick!" cried Mr. Mulroney. "The pond!" He charged straight into the thicket, with the long line of people directly behind him. "Which way?" he cried.

"This way!" said someone.

"Over here!" yelled someone else.

While they were struggling through the undergrowth, Hilary (noticed by no one) sailed gracefully over the treetops. If anyone had been on the other side, they might have seen the kite deposit James smack in the middle of the boating pond, and witnessed his feeble splashing. Then they might have seen Hilary swoop down like an angel out of the sky, seize him by the collar, and drag him to the edge of the pond. But nobody did — they were all too busy trying to find their way through the trees. By the time they emerged, it was all over. The kite was undulating on the water like a great big grinning jellyfish, and James was sitting on the shore coughing and spluttering. Hilary was standing nearby, fastening the toggles on her duffle coat.

"James!" cried Mrs. Mulroney, rushing forward and wrapping her cardigan around him. "Are you all right? What happened?"

But before he could reply, Vicky had pushed to the front of the crowd. "I know!" she yelled. "I know what happened!"

"You do?" said Mr. Mulroney.

"Yes!" Vicky pointed at Hilary. "It's her! She . . . she . . ."

"She what?"

Vicky shifted uncomfortably. "She . . . she . . ."

Everyone stared at her.

"She, um . . ."

Then suddenly, in front of all those people, Vicky's nerve failed. She looked at the ground. "She pulled him out," she said softly.

"*Hooray!*" cried the crowd, and they

hoisted Hilary onto their shoulders and carried her back through the trees, singing.

Vicky trailed behind them, sulking and whacking at flowers with a stick.

When they got back to the car, James was wrapped in the picnic blanket and served hot tea from the thermos while Mrs. Mulroney rubbed his back vigorously to get his circulation going.

"He'll survive," said Mr. Mulroney.

"Yes — thanks to Hilary!" said Mrs. Mulroney. "You've got a guardian angel, James!" she teased. "We'll be forever grateful to her, won't we?"

"Yes," mumbled James.

"What do you say, James?" prompted Mr. Mulroney.

"Thank you, Hilary."

"That's all right," said Hilary. She settled back with a smug expression and hummed softly to herself all the way home. Vicky, on

the other hand, sat in the opposite corner
with her arms folded and didn't say another
word to Hilary or to the twins for the rest of
her stay. And she didn't say much to Mr. and
Mrs. Mulroney, either.

14
Hilary Goes Home

After Vicky left, there came one of those heavy gray days with an iron gust to the air like when it's going to snow. Christmas was only a week away, and the twins were busy wrapping presents and signing cards.

"I'm glad Vicky's gone," said James. "I like it best when we're on our own."

"Yes," said Amanda. "I don't *mind* having guests, but sometimes they stay too long."

"Much too long," agreed James.

Hilary was thoughtful. "How long is too long?" she asked.

"Depends on the person," said James.

"Have *I* stayed too long?"

"Of course not!" cried Amanda. "What makes you think that?"

"Oh! Nothing," said Hilary.

The twins returned to their wrapping, but Hilary sat twiddling with a piece of ribbon, thinking faraway thoughts.

"I suppose it's time I was getting back," she said after a while.

"Back *home?*" said Amanda.

"Yes."

"But I thought you were staying with *us* for Christmas," said Amanda, crestfallen.

"Nah," said Hilary. She twisted the bit of ribbon around her finger. "I have to open all my presents."

James and Amanda exchanged a glance. "You have Christmas, too?" said James.

"Of course!" said Hilary. But she didn't look at them. "I get so many presents it sometimes takes me a week to unwrap them all!"

"But I thought —"

"Yep," Hilary continued. "Christmas is *huge* back home. All the games — and the stories. Wow!" She rolled her eyes.

"Well," said James, "I suppose you'll be glad to get back, then."

"Yep."

But Hilary seemed a little melancholy and didn't say much for the rest of the evening. And later, when the twins went downstairs to decorate the tree, Hilary climbed out onto the roof and sat beside the chimney, hugging her knees and gazing at the stars.

"Aren't you coming in?" asked James when they came back up to the bedroom.

"Not yet," said Hilary.

James left the skylight open for her. "Hilary's very quiet," he remarked, switching off the bedside light.

"Yes," said Amanda. "I thought she was

140

staying with us for Christmas. She never mentioned going home before."

"No," said James.

There was silence while they both lay in the dark, thinking.

"I think she made it up," said Amanda eventually.

"Made what up?"

"About the presents. I bet they don't even *have* presents where she comes from."

"Then why would she say they do?"

"She doesn't want us to feel sorry for her."

"Well, that's silly," said James. "Why doesn't she just stay with us?"

"Maybe she thinks she's outstayed her welcome."

James was quiet for a moment. "Well, we'll tell her we *want* her to stay," he said firmly, "when she comes back in."

"OK," said Amanda.

But before long the twins were sound asleep, their double breaths rising and falling in the darkness. And while they slept, Hilary slipped back through the skylight and closed it very gently so as not to wake them. But she didn't go to bed — she took off her duffle coat and folded it carefully, then took off her sandals and socks and arranged them next to the sofa. Then she tiptoed across the room and crept softly down the stairs.

The house was quiet. The hall clock was tocking peacefully, and the boiler gurgled somewhere far away. Hilary tiptoed into the front room and stopped short, clapping a hand to her mouth. . . . For there, standing in the bay window, was the Christmas tree. The tiny lights cast a speckled pattern around the walls. Little red apples and silver stars and papier-mâché bells hung from the tips of the branches — and there were things the twins had made at school: painted pinecones and paper snowflakes. Hilary crept up to the tree and touched a tiny gold parcel wrapped with a bow. It swung gently.

Hilary turned her attention to the heap of

presents beneath the tree . . . big ones, small ones, all in different patterned paper. She squatted to read the name tags, but the scribbles all looked the same to her. Then she noticed that one of the tags had a picture on it instead of writing: a picture of a stick figure with a triangle for a dress and two big wings. Hilary gave a muffled cry of astonishment — here was a present especially for her!

Hilary had never opened a present before. As quickly as she could she ripped off the paper and found inside a pair of thick red socks and matching mittens and a long red scarf with tassels on the end. She put them all on and stepped back to take one last look at the tree — and that was when she saw it.

At the tip-top of the tree was a small doll in a white dress. It had bare feet and windswept hair, and a pair of feathered wings spread out behind. Hilary clapped her mittens in delight and the tree lights blurred through her tears. For there in pride of place at the top of the Christmas tree, was *Hilary herself*! Hilary smiled. Now she knew that James and Amanda wouldn't forget her.

When the twins awoke it was morning, and their mother was calling.

"Eight o'clock! Breakfast!"

The twins jumped straight out of bed, as you do when the first thing you remember is that it's winter break and nearly Christmas. They were already dressed and heading for the stairs before they realized that Hilary had gone. Amanda's old brown duffle coat lay folded neatly on the sofa, and the sandals sat together on the floor.

"Maybe she's on the roof," said James. He opened the skylight — but there was nobody out there. "Hilary?" he cried, flinging open the closet. But inside there was nothing but clothes hanging silently and a few squashed shoes — and under the beds he found nothing but dust and a couple of feathers. "She can't have just *gone*," he cried.

But it appeared that she had. A heavy silence seemed to fill the whole house; it felt very empty without her.

"I bet there's a big demand for guardian angels," said Amanda soberly. "Especially at this time of year."

"But we never even said good-bye!"

"No."

"Wait a minute!" James had noticed something. He rushed to the sofa and pulled a piece of paper out from under the pillow. "What's this?"

"A note! What does it say?"

"Nothing," said James, disappointed. "It's only pictures."

But Amanda took it from him. "It *does* say something," she said. "Look!"

And so it did.

It can get cold flying at night, even when you're wearing woolly red socks and mittens. And tonight is a crisp, clear night and the rooftops are silvered with frost. There goes Hilary now! Off she flies, full of the cheerful satisfaction of the accomplished do-gooder — skimming across the tiles with her red socks kicking and her red scarf streaming out behind her like a banner. Oops! She nearly snagged her scarf on that chimney stack. "Careful, Hilary! Chimneys can be dangerous!" But I'm not sure she can hear us now — she's too far away.

"Bye, Hilary! Until next time!"

Hilary's note says: I will be back.